The
JASON KIDD
Story

by

David Moore

SCHOLASTIC INC.
New York Toronto London Auckland Sydney

Photo Credits: Book
Cover, 10, 53, Back Cover: NBA/Glenn James. **6, 57, 61:** NBA/Layne Murdoch. **13:** NBA/Andy Hayt. **16, 20, 24, 28:** Photos courtesy of Anne Kidd. **33:** NBA/ Richard Mukai. **38:** NBA/Ron Hoskins. **44, 75:** NBA/Andrew D. Bernstein. **49:** NBA/Jerry Wachter. **65:** NBA/Fernando Medina. **66:** NBA/Scott Cunningham. **69:** NBA/Jon Hayt.

Photo Credits: Insert Section
I, IV, VIII: NBA/Layne Murdoch. **II:** NBA/Noren Trotman. **III:** NBA/Glenn James. **V, VII:** NBA/Andy Hayt. **VI:** NBA/Richard Lewis.

If you purchased this book without a cover, you should be aware that this book is stolen property. It was reported as "unsold and destroyed" to the publisher, and neither the author nor the publisher has received payment for this "stripped book."

No part of this publication may be reproduced in whole or in part, or stored in a retrieval system, or transmitted in any form or by any means, electronic, mechanical, photocopying, recording, or otherwise, without written permission of the publisher. For information regarding permission, write to Scholastic Inc., 555 Broadway, New York, NY 10012.

The NBA and individual NBA member team identifications are trademarks, copyrighted designs, and other forms of intellectual property of NBA Properties, Inc. and the respective member teams and may not be used without the prior written consent of NBA Properties, Inc. All rights reserved.

ISBN 0-590-13772-7

© 1997 by NBA Properties, Inc.
All rights reserved. Published by Scholastic Inc.

12 11 10 9 8 7 6 5 4 3 2   7 8 9/9 0 1 2/0

Printed in the U.S.A.
First Scholastic printing, February 1997
Book design: Gewirtz Graphics, Inc.

*To Kelsey, may you never lose your curiosity
and enthusiasm
—D. M.*

TABLE OF CONTENTS

The moment Jason first stepped on the court, he became one of the NBA's brightest new stars.

chapter one

NTRODUCTION

The rubber band fits snug around his right wrist.

Jason Kidd has worn one of these since junior high. It is his way of staying in touch with his roots.

"I call it my reality check," Jason said. "It's just a reminder to me that I'm supposed to be having fun and enjoying life. It works on good days, but it's better on bad ones. It helps me keep my head on straight."

There are more good days than bad. Kidd isn't just another basketball player in the NBA. He is a star. The Dallas Mavericks point guard is one of the game's best young players. Kidd shared the NBA Schick Rookie of the Year Award with Detroit's Grant Hill in 1995. He is the only Dallas player to ever start in the NBA All-Star Game.

In a very short time, Kidd has earned the respect of his teammates, coaches, and some of the sport's greatest stars. Bob Cousy is a Hall of Fame point guard who played for the Boston Celtics in the 1950s and early '60s. He says Kidd's instincts are unbelievable and that he has a natural feel for the game.

The rubber band around Jason's wrist is a reminder that he's supposed to **have fun and enjoy life.**

"I don't say this about a lot of NBA players today," Cousy said, "but I'd pay to see Kidd play."

Charles Barkley and Earvin "Magic" Johnson say the same thing. Johnson raves about Kidd's enthusiasm and talks about his ability to create shots for his teammates. Barkley says Kidd is good for the game and one of his favorite players to watch. Barkley believes Kidd could become one of the best players in the NBA.

"I think that Jason Kidd is one of the most advanced and talented players to come into the league in a long time," Barkley said. "He and Anfernee Hardaway might be the best rookies in the last ten years. They're the only ones who came in with complete games."

Shining Star

The Mavericks joke about the mobs that swarm Kidd when he's out in public. Former teammate, forward Popeye Jones, remembers when he and Kidd made an appearance at an electronics store last season. Jones said when the appearance was over, fans followed their limo hoping to find out where Kidd lived.

"It's like traveling with a rock band," Jones said.

Kidd has shot commercials for Nike and ESPN. He has attended the MTV awards. He has appeared on *The Tonight Show with Jay Leno*.

The Kidd Club—a fan club devoted to the twenty-three-year-old star—has more than 1,000 members. Kidd's advisors say the athlete receives an average of 375 pieces of mail a week during the season. In Dallas, kids of all ages wear replicas of his No. 5 jersey. While in high school, Jason had more stories written about him in the *San Francisco Chronicle* than former 49ers quarterback Joe Montana.

Despite all the acclaim, Jason remained down-to-earth. "I never thought of him as a superstar," said Jason's sister, Denise. "He was just a brother."

Kidd grew up in a lower-middle class neighborhood outside of Oakland, California. His father, Steve, was a supervisor with TWA airlines. His mother, Anne, was a banker. Jason also has two

Jason runs the Mavericks offense with an unselfish attitude. Jason would rather make a great pass than take a shot.

younger sisters, Denise and Kimberly.

Steve Kidd often flies around the country to watch his son play. Jason remains close to his family and refers to them "as my cement."

There is so much attention, so many demands, on Kidd's time. Sometimes, snapping that rubber band around his wrist isn't enough. Sometimes, he needs more to snap back to reality. This is when he turns to his family. They help him keep it all in perspective. What Kidd doesn't want is to become so big he can't enjoy the little things. While Jason appreciates his enormous popularity, he is also wary of the many problems that come along with superstardom in the NBA.

"The attention has been there as long as I can remember," Kidd said. "It's like a part of me. I think it will always be there.

"I'm never going to be bigger than life. If I can't go to the movies with other people, then there's a problem. If I can't go to the mall with other people, then there's really something wrong. I mean, that's not being human and that's not going to make you feel good inside if you want to separate yourself from other people.

"People know they can see me and talk to me and shake my hand and not worry about having a whole entourage around me telling them, 'No, he's not talking to you.' "

Student of the Game

Kidd studies everything about his opponent. Tendencies. Facial expressions. Body language. Breathing patterns. If the player is too pumped up, Kidd has found the player looks to shoot, not pass.

"I'm playing defense thinking, 'Does he want to pass, or does he really want to shoot the ball?'" Kidd said. "I'll look in his eyes, then lay off and play for the steal. Sometimes, he'll outguess me, and he'll shoot because he's open, and coach might yell at me. But I know nine times out of ten, I can outguess my opponent."

"Jason is a true student of the game," said Todd Bozeman, Kidd's coach at the University of California. "He watches game film, studies his opponent's tendencies, breaks down the other team's plays. He's able to see the game differently than most."

Teammates say the more you see Kidd, the more you appreciate what he can do. The great passes make the highlight tapes. The triple-double—double figures in three of the following categories: points, rebounds, assists, blocked shots, or steals—jump out of the box scores.

But what fans don't see are the hustle plays that help the Mavericks win games. They don't see the key rebound or pass that leads to a victory. They don't see the key steal or the time-out that is called

Jason's size and strength allow him to fearlessly take the ball to the hole.

as he's about to fall out-of-bounds.

Fresno coach Jerry Tarkanian dubbed Kidd "the next Magic Johnson" when he played for California. What does the original Magic Johnson have to say about Kidd?

> **"I love his attitude.**
>
> *He'll make a great pass...then hustles back to play defense. I love it."*
> **—Magic Johnson**

"I love his attitude," Johnson said. "He'll make a great pass that finds a teammate free for a dunk, then he hustles back to play defense. I love it.

"Jason is a creator. He creates people's shots, where OK, the defense is back, it's four on four, now Jason's going to make you do something, commit, and then he's going to get the guy a shot. See, that's the difference. You've got a lot of guys who can run the offense and run it well, but you don't have guys who can create a shot for different people. Jason can create shots."

Kidd's goal is to make the game fun for his teammates. He learned that from watching Johnson.

"I will probably always pattern my game after Magic Johnson," Kidd said. "He was a total player. He always had fun on the court but, at the same time, he took care of business and he made everybody better around him. He brought his team to another level."

The NBA has lost some of the star power that has helped it burn so bright. Johnson and Boston's Larry Bird have retired. Chicago's Michael Jordan doesn't plan to play much longer. It is time for the league to turn its future over to a new generation.

Kidd is part of that movement.

"I think it's time that the league gets a shot in the arm by having youth pick up the slack," Kidd said. "I hope I can be part of that."

A future NBA superstar — Jason Kidd in second grade.

chapter two

GROWING UP

Jason Frederick Kidd didn't always dream of playing in the NBA.

A cowboy. That's what Jason wanted to be when he grew up. He loved actor John Wayne. At the age of three, Jason would sit in front of the TV and watch every old western that came on the screen.

The Kidd family had three horses. Jason's parents, Steve and Anne, took him out one afternoon to ride an Appaloosa named Suki in the hills around Oakland. They warned him to go slow.

Jason didn't listen. John Wayne wouldn't go slow. Why should Jason? He soon discovered the answer.

"Just when I got going, a dog ran out and spooked Suki," Jason remembered. "He raised up and bucked me off, and that was it. My riding career was over. I knew it was time to use my own two feet."

It didn't take long for Jason to turn his attention from horses to athletics. His parents laugh now when they recall how he always seemed to have a ball in his hands or at his feet. Football. Basketball. Baseball. Soccer. Jason played them all. If either parent had a task to do, they knew they could always stick a ball in front of Jason and keep him happy.

In the fifth grade, Jason had to make a choice:

basketball

or

soccer?

"We were just keeping him occupied," Anne said. "We knew he was coordinated from the time he was an infant. But we never really thought wow, he could be a star."

A Star Is Born

The older Jason got, the more crazy weekends became around the Kidd household. Soccer practice in the morning. Baseball practice in the afternoon. A trip down to the park to shoot baskets. Jason's parents found themselves driving their son all over town.

One of the first signs that Jason was a special athlete came in the fourth grade. He scored 21 of his team's 30 points in a Catholic League game. One of the first signs of Jason's toughness came a few weeks later.

It was Thanksgiving afternoon. Jason and a few other kids in the neighborhood got together to play football. A few minutes into the game, Jason got behind his defender and went deep. As soon as the ball touched his hands, he crashed into a mailbox.

"I thought I had broken my jaw," Jason said. "But I held onto the ball, went inside for a drink, and went back out to finish the game."

Soccer was his first love. Jason was a promising forward. But the schedules for soccer and basketball conflicted while he was in fifth grade. He had to choose.

Jay Hadnot was one of Jason's best friends. Jay's father, Jimmy Hadnot, is Jason's godfather.

Jay convinced Jason to give up soccer for basketball. But he didn't stop there. Every day after school, Hadnot would drop by Jason's house to play basketball. The two would join friends Andre Cornwell and Kris Stone for the ride down the hill to Grass Valley Elementary.

The court was cement and had eight-foot rims. That's where Jason learned the game.

Most of the players on that court were older than

One day Jason would have to make a choice between two loves —
basketball and soccer.

Jason. Hadnot was four years older. Jason was the scrub, the last player picked almost every time. But he got better. He also learned the more he passed, the higher he was picked.

"It was intimidating to play with them, but Jay made me," Jason said. "I was just out there for exercise at first, but he taught me how to pass and who to pass to. He helped me develop my joy for passing."

Born: March 23, 1973

Favorite Actor: Robert DeNiro

Favorite Actress: Julia Roberts

ODDS AND ENDS

Favorite Recording Artists:
Isley Brothers and Chante Moore

Favorite Food: Chinese

Shoe Size: 13-and-a-half

One Thing Would Most Like to Do:
"Make a hole in one."

Pet: Rottweiler named Mia given to him by former Texas A&M football star Sam Adams

What Jason didn't know at the time was that Hadnot developed an addiction to drugs. A few years later, in 1990, Jay Hadnot checked out of a drug rehabilitation center. He killed himself a short time after leaving. He was twenty-one years old. Jason still becomes emotional when talking about his friend.

> **"Jay taught me a lot of lessons.**
>
> *Showing me what can happen if you decide to use drugs was one of them."*
> —*Jason Kidd*

"Jay taught me a lot of lessons," Jason said. "Showing me what can happen if you decide to use drugs was one of them.

"He was my older brother. I always looked up to him. He pushed me and he always took the time to be with me. I will remember him."

Cornwell said Hadnot's death made Kidd, "work real hard toward life, toward being a better person. Life is not a game, and that was reiterated in the incident. I think it made him more mature."

On that cement court with the eight-foot rims, Jason matured quickly. He and Cornwell would stay late and work on plays. They would watch Johnson and Kareem Abdul-Jabbar with the Los Angeles Lakers and try to mimic their give-and-go play. Soon, kids in the neighborhood began to hear about the passing skills of this precocious sixth grader.

"About that time everybody started saying how great Jason was," said his father, Steve. "We were flattered but a little afraid to accept it. But by high school, there was no doubt he was going to be something special."

Kidd began to receive letters from major college programs while he was still in junior high. He was signing autographs by the time he was fourteen.

"But he never got the big head," said his sister, Denise. "I hung out with him and the guys. He picked on me but let me hang around. He never acted like a superstar."

The summer before his freshman year at St. Joseph of Notre Dame High School, Jason took part in a pickup game with some college players. The gym was packed. Lou Campanelli, then the head coach at California, was one of the spectators.

Immediately, his eyes were drawn to Jason. He turned to Frank LaPorte, the coach at St. Joseph's, and began to ask some questions.

"Even then, you could tell Jason was more than special," LaPorte said. "Lou leaned over to me and asked about the new kid, thinking he was a junior or senior transfer. When I told him he was an eighth grader, he about fell off the bleachers."

Jason benefitted from a close, supportive family. Here he is at age twelve.

chapter three

HIGH SCHOOL

The door to LaPorte's office swings open and reveals a museum.

One wall features a "Whiz Kidd" poster of the best player in St. Joseph's history. Adjacent to that exhibit hangs a watercolor of the same poster. Another wall is plastered with pictures of the point guard. Kidd passing. Kidd dunking. Kidd grinning.

Kidd winning. Most of the plaques in LaPorte's office are related to the two state championships St. Joseph's won while Kidd was at the school. He led the team to a 122–14 record in his four years and became the most celebrated high school player in the country.

"Jason put our school on the map," LaPorte said. "Once we had 5,000 fans at a game. When I took

Jason out with four minutes left, 4,999 got up and walked out."

An exaggeration? Sure. But that is the stuff of legends.

St. Joseph of Notre Dame is a private school with an enrollment of just under 600. The school is nestled in Alameda, nine miles from the neighborhood in which Kidd grew up. The gym seats 750. But that was a waste of Kidd's drawing power. LaPorte had certain games moved to California State-Hayward or the Oakland Coliseum. Those games regularly pulled in roughly 11,000 fans.

People came from all over to see Kidd's mesmerizing talent. One graduate of the high school was a highway patrolman in Nevada. LaPorte talked about how that man would make the three-and-a-half hour drive just to see Kidd play. He never missed a game.

"He was head and shoulders above everyone," LaPorte said. "We sold out every game. You couldn't get a seat in our place for twenty-five dollars, and they were suposed to go for five dollars. I had more friends than I've ever had. They were hanging on the walls outside the gym, looking in through the window."

Kidd's reputation followed the team on the road. LaPorte was reluctant to remove Kidd too early when St. Joseph was on the road because the crowd would become disappointed and upset.

LaPorte didn't let this star power go to waste. The school sold Kidd caps, T-shirts, and posters. An autographed basketball by Kidd once brought $750 at an auction. A set of three autographed balls at another fund-raiser netted $1,500. The team sold doughnuts in the gym before school to raise money.

Once, LaPorte asked Kidd to sign 250 rubber basketballs to raise enough money for the team to go on an out-of-state trip. Every single ball sold at a pancake breakfast sponsored by the school.

Jason led St. Joseph's to a 122–14 record *over the course of four years.*

One of those trips was to Arkansas. After the game, a woman approached Kidd. She introduced herself then shoved a girl in Kidd's direction.

"This is my daughter," the woman said. "I hope you marry her someday."

Compared to that, the autograph requests from Ohio and Florida seemed tame.

"I can't describe what it was like," LaPorte said. "Watching him play, or even practice, was like a spiritual event. People wanted to see the kid make something so impossible look effortless."

Jason poses for the camera as a high school freshman. Jason was already attracting the attention of college scouts across the nation.

A Special Bond

LaPorte and Kidd remain close. Kidd says, "He's ninety-nine percent of the reason I'm the player and person I am today."

LaPorte responds, "I love him like a son."

It was LaPorte who helped trumpet the Kidd legend. By the time Kidd finished high school, a Bay Area paper concluded he was the best player ever to come out of northern California. Better, even, than former Boston Celtics star Bill Russell.

"That is a very strong statement," Kidd said. "Just to be mentioned in that company is an honor."

Several national publications ranked Kidd as the No. 1 recruit in the country his senior year. He was the California Player of the Year his junior and senior seasons when he led St. Joseph to the state title. Kidd finished his high school career with more assists than any player in California prep history. He averaged 25 points, 10 assists, 7 rebounds, and 7 steals as a senior. That earned him the Naismith Award as the nation's top high school player.

Parade magazine and *USA Today* were just two of the national publications that declared Kidd High School Player of the Year. He was such big news that his SAT scores were on the front page of the Oakland newspaper.

Kidd promised LaPorte a car if he became the top-recruited player in the country. When that hap-

DIAMOND VISION

Jason carries a rookie baseball card of Seattle's Ken Griffey Jr. with him. "Junior is the best in baseball," Jason said. "My goal is to be the best in basketball."

pened, Kidd autographed a picture of himself. It reads, "To Coach—Thanks for the support." In the bottom left-hand corner, there is a drawing of a car with the message "That's next" scribbled over it.

LaPorte drives a 1980 Thunderbird. But he has always dreamed of owning a Cadillac El Dorado with a maroon interior.

"I couldn't draw a Cadillac," Kidd said. "But I promised it to him, and I'm gonna hold to that."

chapter four

COLLEGE YEARS

Some would call it a "hair-brained" scheme. But Kidd wanted to give it a shot. The thought of walking around campus without having to stop to sign autographs was one that appealed to him.

So Kidd went to work. He devoted every second of every day to his goal of growing a beard.

"I'm trying to grow a beard so I can keep a low profile," Kidd said.

It didn't work. Fans were fooled for a day or two. But Kidd was one of the most recognized athletes in the Bay Area. He was one of the best players in college basketball. Low profile, he wasn't. He eventually shaved and accepted his fate.

What Kidd did in two short years at the University of California was remarkable. He resurrected a program that had been dormant for nearly thirty years. He was such a draw that the school moved several of its home games from the campus gym to the Oakland Coliseum. Only 6,578 people could see Kidd play at Harmon Gym. Roughly 15,000 could witness his talent at the Coliseum.

In the words of Golden Bears coach Todd Bozeman, Kidd had charisma. Bozeman watched as fans chased his star player night and day. The athletic department eventually moved Kidd off campus to give him a little privacy.

Bozeman said, "When we were at Washington for a game, I was straightening my tie in a mirror when some guy jumped out of a locker behind me with an autograph book. People can't imagine the things we went through daily.

"All eyes were on him, and he produced spectacular results night in and night out."

Freshman Sensation

Kidd led the Golden Bears to their first national ranking in more than thirty years. He averaged 13 points, 7.7 assists and led the nation in steals with an average of 3.8. His 110 thefts broke the NCAA record set by his good friend, Gary Payton.

Four publications named Kidd the Freshman of the Year in college basketball. He played a major role in Cal's second-round upset of Duke in the 1993

Thanks to Jason's leadership, the California Golden Bears became a force in the college ranks.

NCAA Tournament. But not everything about that first season went smoothly.

The Golden Bears stumbled to a 10–7 start. That disappointing performance, amidst such high expectations, led to the dismissal of coach Lou Campanelli and the hiring of assistant coach Bozeman.

California won 11-of-13 games under Bozeman. The team finished the season with a 21–9 record and placed second in the Pac-10. It also advanced to the Sweet 16 for the first time since 1960.

Bozeman called Kidd, "the most competitive person I've ever been around." He talked about Kidd's talent, but stressed there was much more. Bozeman maintained Kidd enjoyed the success he did because he worked so hard.

That hard work paid off in the NCAA Tournament. Kidd hit a twisting layup with 1.5 seconds left to lead California to a 66–64 first-round victory over LSU. Tigers coach Dale Brown dubbed it, "the pretzel shot."

Two nights later, Kidd's three-point play with 1:11 remaining keyed the team's 82–77 victory over defending champion Duke. That basket ended the Blue Devils bid to win a third consecutive title.

"I think they needed a play like that at that point," Duke coach Mike Krzyzewski said. "It's one of those plays that kids like him will make."

There weren't enough plays from Kidd or his teammates to get past Kansas. But the Golden Bears served notice they were now a basketball power. Bay Area fans looked forward to an encore performance.

The Legend Grows

Six national magazines rated California as one of the top eight teams in the country entering the 1993–94 season. Kidd simply rated the Golden Bears as a Top 20 team. But he did predict Cal would win the Pac-10 championship and advance to the Final Four in Charlotte.

Kidd returned for his second season a stronger player. An improved player. The point guard added ten pounds of muscle to tip the scales at 205 pounds. He played for the U.S. team during the summer in its tour against European National teams. Kidd didn't let the publicity—he made the cover of *Sports Illustrated* as a freshman—go to his head.

"I worked hard last season at Cal and I worked hard in the offseason," Kidd said. "I like to think the attention I'm getting comes from that. My parents save the magazines and the articles, but I don't pay too much attention to them.

"A lot of people have been in the situation I'm in.

Many have been successful, but some have fallen by the wayside. I just want to make sure that doesn't happen."

Kidd sometimes struggled with his classes. But he rarely struggled on the court. He approached basketball practice as his laboratory. He would experiment. Behind-the-back passes. One-hand bounce passes on the run. Kidd was always looking for better ways to get the ball to his teammates.

Jason was such a great passer, his teammates came up with an explanation: **He had eyes in the back of his head.**

Some of those experiments would blow up in Kidd's face. Most of the time, they worked.

"I think coach is more comfortable that I will make the right decision," Kidd said. "As long as he is comfortable and doesn't have a heart attack, then I'll be all right."

Bozeman noticed an improvement in Kidd's ability to control a game his sophomore season. He regarded Kidd as "a born leader." But Bozeman said Kidd also understood he didn't have to take everything upon himself. He worked to get his teammates involved. He also worked on the one noticeable flaw in his game—the outside shot.

"Once I can consistently make that jump shot from twelve to fifteen feet, the defensive player is going to be at my mercy," Kidd said.

"The misconception is Jason can't shoot," Bozeman said. "They said the same thing about Magic Johnson. They said the same thing about Michael Jordan. If he was a complete player, then why would he need college?"

Teammates talked about how Kidd had eyes in the back of his head. Forward Lamond Murray was quick to credit Kidd for his high scoring average. Early in the season, when California knocked off No. 1 ranked UCLA, Oregon State coach Jim Anderson said, "the last five mintues of that game, Jason played as well as anyone I've seen in the last five years." Kidd finished the game with 18 points, 14 rebounds, and 12 assists.

The praise didn't stop there. Washington State coach Kelvin Sampson, who later went to Oklahoma, called Kidd the most disruptive player in the Pac-10 since Gary Payton. Washington coach Bob Bender said his appreciation for Kidd grew every time he watched him play in person.

"You'd like not to like him for whatever reason because he's so good," Stanford coach Mike Montgomery said. "But I can't do that. I just really admire him because of the way he plays and his competitive spirit.

After being selected second overall by the Dallas Mavericks in the 1994 NBA Draft, Jason was congratulated by NBA Commissioner David Stern.

"I don't know if you can exploit his deficiencies because he has such a presence on the court. He rarely complains about a call. He acknowledges when he makes a mistake, even when it's maybe not his fault. He makes the plays at the end of the game. Kidd, in many ways, is in a category by himself in his impact on the game."

Kidd averaged 16.7 points, 9.1 assists, 6.9 rebounds, and 3.1 steals his sophomore season. He led the nation in assists. He had four triple-doubles. The coaches named him the Pac-10 Player of the Year, the first time the award had ever been given to a sophomore. Kidd became the only player in school history to receive that honor. He was a consensus All-American, named to the first team on 64 of 65 ballots. The last Golden Bear selected as first team All-American was Darrell Imhoff in 1960.

All in all, it was a successful regular season. But California didn't play well in the final five games. The team finished 22–7 for the season and fell into second place in the conference. Kidd's confidence wasn't shaken. He promised the Golden Bears wouldn't overlook Wisconsin-Green Bay in the first round of the NCAA Tournament and again said he expected the team to advance to the Final Four.

They didn't. Wisconsin-Green Bay stunned Cal in the first round.

Kidd had provided a jump start for the California

program. He broke the school's career assists and steals records in just two seasons. In a very short period, Kidd's name became associated with California basketball. But there were persistent rumors that the point guard was prepared to move on to the NBA.

"I'm just going to be happy for as long as I have an opportunity to coach Jason, because not a lot of people will be able to say that," Bozeman said. "I think he's going to end up being one of the all-time great players."

chapter five

AKING THE JUMP

The first two minutes were smooth. Kidd didn't cry. His voice didn't crack once as he announced he was leaving the University of California for the NBA.

But when Kidd said good-bye to his teammates, it started. Tears streamed down his face. Bozeman, sitting next to his point guard, began to cry as well.

"I told you not to do that," Bozeman said.

"I tried not to," Kidd replied.

Kidd's father, Steve, handed the pair some Kleenex. The two wiped their eyes and continued.

It was an emotional day. Jason Kidd, on his twenty-first birthday, was ready to make the jump. After two successful years at California, the sophomore was leaving for the NBA Draft.

A few months earlier, Kidd had declared he wouldn't leave the school until it made the Final Four. The Golden Bears fell short of that goal. Still, no one questioned if Kidd was making the right decision. The absence of bitter feelings was a tribute to his talent and popularity. After all, Kidd had done for California what he had done for St. Joseph's High School—put it on the basketball map.

"He's been destined for the NBA *since he could walk."* **—Gary Payton**

Reporters packed the Hall of Fame room at the university to chronicle Kidd's decision. Bozeman turned the tables on the reporters. He asked them if they had the chance to be a columnist at a major newspaper after just two years in school, would they take it or would they return to school?

"Wouldn't you take it if you were in fact ready?" Bozeman asked. "Well, that's the case with Jason. Last year, I wasn't sure he was ready. This year, yes. I mean, he could stay three more years and he might not be any more prepared than he is now."

Gregg Popovich agreed. An assistant coach with the Golden State Warriors, Popovich saw Kidd more than most in the NBA. He proved to be one of Kidd's staunchest supporters.

"He has tremendous explosiveness and a great desire to win," said Popovich, now the executive vice president of basketball operations with the San Antonio Spurs. "You have to understand that the best players in the world play in the NBA, yet Jason would be at the upper end of those players in pure explosiveness.

"He has the desire to dominate, actually to destroy an opponent. I believe he'll be a superstar in the NBA. Maybe I'm overstating it, but I don't think so."

Kidd left the Golden Bears, but he didn't forget. The *Oakland Tribune* sponsored a video of Kidd's highlights. The tape sold for $19.99. The proceeds benefitted the Jason Kidd Basketball Scholarship Fund at California.

NBA Bound

Kidd's legend among NBA players was actually established before he ever went to college. He played in a Pro-Am League the summer before his freshman year. Several NBA players took part. Seattle's Gary Payton and Brian Shaw, then with Miami, were two of them.

Kidd's exposure to these players wasn't limited to games. He often practiced against Payton and Shaw. He played pickup games with them.

Payton and Shaw did this to stay in shape. Kidd

Long hours in the gym helped make Jason a star. Today, he still works just as hard to improve all aspects of his game.

did this to see if he was good enough to play in the NBA. Payton and Shaw were the measuring sticks.

"When they're beating me bad in one-on-one, they'll rub it in saying, 'You're not ready,'" Kidd said. "They give me a hard time. I know I have a lot to learn, and I don't mind learning, because I'm always looking to be one step ahead of the next person."

He learned quickly. Kidd was the Most Valuable Player of the Pro-Am League that summer before his freshman year. Payton and Shaw may have been older and better. But Kidd was improving. Fast.

"He's been destined for the NBA since he could walk," Payton said.

Simply playing in the NBA wasn't enough for Kidd. It was expected. He wanted more.

That became clear in the days leading up to the draft. There was no question Kidd would be among the first three players taken. All signs appeared to point to him landing in Dallas with the No. 2 pick. A few hours before he was selected, Kidd talked about his standards.

"A lot of hard work has been put into this, but I'm not satisfied with just being here," Kidd said. "I hope I can push on and be an All-Star and then, hopefully, a legend in this game. But I have a long way to go. I have a lot to learn about the game of basketball. Right now, I'm just being a sponge and trying to absorb it all."

Jason Kidd and Earvin "Magic" Johnson both left school after their sophomore seasons. Here's a comparison of what the two did in their final college season.

POINT-COUNTERPOINT

Kidd
16.7 points
6.9 rebounds
9.1 assists
47.2 percent from
the field

Johnson
17.1 points
7.3 rebounds
8.4 assists
46.8 percent from
the field

What about his immediate goals?

"For the first year, it's to be Rookie of the Year," Kidd said. "And to be in the top five in steals and assists. Those are just personal goals. Teamwise, I want to add fifteen to twenty games to the winning percentage. I also would like to bring a winning attitude to the team, to show some leadership. That's probably about it for my first year."

When asked if there was anything else, Kidd got a sheepish grin.

"Well," he said, realizing his lofty goals, "that's a whole lot."

chapter six

ROOKIE OF THE YEAR

The Mavericks cap sat in the back of Anne Kidd's car for several years. It seemed out of place. Not many kids in the Bay Area followed a team from Dallas. But Jason borrowed the hat from a friend one day and never returned it.

"I liked it because green is my favorite color," Kidd said. "But I also saw myself playing in Dallas for some reason."

Teammates rave about Kidd's instincts. Here was another example. Dallas used the second pick of the 1994 NBA Draft to select Kidd. The club chose him ahead of Duke's Grant Hill.

Dallas came within one victory of advancing to the NBA Finals in 1988. After that, the franchise hit hard times. The Mavericks won just 11 games during the 1992–93 season. The team had to win the final two games of the season to avoid tying the worst record in league history. Dallas followed that with 13 victories the next season.

Attendance was down. So was morale. The club needed a shot in the arm.

It turned out to be Kidd.

"My mom told me she needs a new cap because it's faded," Jason said at his first Mavericks press conference. "I guess now I'll get her a new one."

Making a Point

Utah's John Stockton has more assists than any player in NBA history. He spent his first two-and-a-half seasons in the league on the bench behind Ricky Green.

Stockton isn't alone. Very few point guards in the league today stepped in and had an impact their first season. Payton. Kevin Johnson. Mark Price. Kenny Anderson. Rod Strickland. All spent significant time on the bench in their rookie seasons.

"A lot of times you're coming down and you're just wondering," said Price, now a four-time All-Star. "Should I shoot? Should I pass? It takes a little while to get used to all that."

The nuances of the game all come into play at the point guard position. Hall of Fame guard Oscar Robertson said the hardest decision a point guard

Even when he's spectacular, Jason makes the game look easy.

has to make is when to pass and when to shoot. Denver coach Bernie Bickerstaff said all you can do is teach the point guard to execute the plays. You can't teach instincts or innate skill.

"It's difficult for all young players," said Kevin Johnson, a three-time All-Star himself. "But I think it's more difficult for a point guard.

"Most players, it's just going to take them some time. One or two years isn't going to give you the maturity to be a good point guard. I can't say the amount of time. Maybe six or seven years. It might be three or four. It's just a matter of working hard, finding your niche, and finding what you can do effectively and build on that."

Earvin "Magic" Johnson. Isiah Thomas. Those are two points guards over the last sixteen years who hit the court running.

Kidd added his name to that elite group. One week into training camp, Kidd had memorized every play in the Dallas playbook. Not only his responsibilities, but those of the four other positions as well. By the end of camp, the coaching staff marveled at the feel Kidd had for the game. He already knew where his teammates wanted the ball and when they wanted to shoot.

"He makes passes that bring people to games, but he doesn't take a lot of chances," said Dick Motta, who coached Kidd his first two years in the league. "Jason is constantly working on his ball-handling and passing, at practice and on his own. You can't teach that kind of dedication."

First Impression

Opening night came on November 5 at Reunion Arena. A sellout crowd of 17,502 was on hand to see if this new Kidd in town would make a difference.

He did. Kidd had 10 points, 11 assists, and 9 re-bounds in his regular season debut. The Mavericks beat the New Jersey Nets, 112–103.

There was a string of impressive performances for Kidd early in the season. But Grant Hill could make the same claim. The Detroit Pistons took the small forward with the third pick. He averaged more than 20 points a game and electrified crowds with his high-flying style. A fan favorite, Hill started in the All-Star Game after receiving more votes than any other player.

Jason's hard-nosed play and maximum effort *earned him the instant respect of NBA coaches and players.*

Hill was considered the leading candidate for Rookie of the Year. Even Kidd conceded Hill was the favorite. But Jason kept plugging away. And the Mavericks kept winning.

Dallas beat the San Antonio Spurs on the road in December. Kidd played a key role in the victory. His steal of an inbounds pass in the final seconds of regulation—he called a twenty-second timeout in midair before landing out of bounds—gave Dallas the possession they needed to send the game into overtime.

"He's a man," Spurs coach Bob Hill said of Kidd. "He manhandled us, kicked our butts all night. His stats don't mean a thing. He's special. He played like a veteran."

Kidd's all-out play earned instant respect from coaches and players. The rookie was forced to miss two games in February when he checked into the hospital with dehydration and the flu. Kidd kept a wooden stool in his locker all season. He was so exhausted after games, he often sat on the stool to take a shower.

"You can't pace yourself," Kidd said. "You've got to give it your all."

Indiana coach Larry Brown had seen that quality from a young age. Brown met Kidd at the age of thirteen. Jimmy Hadnot, Kidd's godfather, played professional basketball with Brown. Hadnot persuaded Kidd to travel from California to Kansas for Brown's basketball camp one summer.

Usually cool on the court, Jason seems mystified by a referee's call.

Only three rookies in NBA history had a bigger impact on their team's win-loss record than Kidd.

SUDDEN IMPACT

Player	Season	Increase in Wins
David Robinson, San Antonio	1989–90	+35
Larry Bird, Boston	1979–80	+32
Kareem Abdul-Jabbar, Milwaukee	1969–70	+29
Jason Kidd, Dallas	1994–95	+23
Mitch Richmond, Golden State	1988–89	+23
Elvin Hayes, San Diego	1968–69	+22
Shaquille O'Neal, Orlando	1992–93	+20
Hakeem Olajuwon, Houston	1984–85	+19
Isiah Thomas, Detroit	1981–82	+18
Wilt Chamberlain, Philadelphia	1959–60	+17

Note: The Chicago Bulls improved by 11 games in Michael Jordan's first season (1984-85) and the Los Angeles Lakers improved by 13 games and won the NBA Championship in Earvin "Magic" Johnson's first season (1979-80).

"He had terrific skills as a young kid," Brown said. "But ever since I've been watching him, the thing that stands out in my mind is his competitiveness and his love for the game. He seems to play every possession like it's the most important possession. He likes to make his teammates better.

"He is already as good a player as there is in this league. The things he does, the plays he makes, unfortunately, don't measure in the stats. But they make a difference in the outcome of a game. We're lucky as coaches to have someone in this league like Jason."

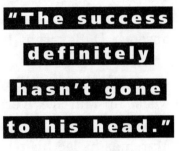

"The success definitely hasn't gone to his head."

—Grant Hill

Strong Finish

Grant Hill missed twelve games with a leg injury. When he returned, he continued his strong play. Milwaukee's Glenn Robinson, the first player taken in the draft, also played well.

But Kidd improved as the season wore on. More and more players and coaches began to talk about him as the Rookie of the Year.

"I know Grant Hill is the latest flava, spelled with an A, but Jason Kidd has all thirty-one flavors," Los Angeles Lakers forward Cedric Ceballos said. "Kidd may have more of an impact on the game than either of the other two guys [Hill or Robinson] because he controls the flow. His impact on the game is amazing, especially for a guy who isn't even shooting the lights out. He does so many other things that won't show up in the boxscore."

Ironically, Kidd's push for Rookie of the Year received a boost when a teammate went down. Guard Jim Jackson suffered a severe ankle sprain on February 24 and never returned. Kidd averaged 15.8 points, 8.2 assists, and 5.3 rebounds in his absence. Dallas went 16–14 during that period.

Kidd clearly took control of the team. He was named the league's Player of the Week for the third week in March, averaging 20 points and 10.5 assists. He was named Rookie of the Month for March as he led his team to a 10–6 mark.

Kidd led the league in triple-doubles with four. All four came in a 16-day span in April. He had 38 points, 11 rebounds, and 10 assists in a victory over the NBA Champion Houston Rockets on April 11.

The season ended with Kidd averaging 11.7 points, 7.7 assists, and 5.4 rebounds. He was the only rookie to finish among the league leaders in two categories—assists (7.7 tied for ninth) and steals (1.91 was seventh). A few weeks later, Kidd shared the NBA Schick Rookie of the Year Award with Hill. Each player received 43 first-place votes out of 105 cast.

Jason shared 1995 NBA Schick Rookie of the Year honors with Detroit's remarkable forward Grant Hill.

This was just the fourth tie in the forty-nine-year history of the award. Boston's Dave Cowens and Portland's Geoff Petrie shared the honor in '70–71, Indianapolis' Bill Tosheff and Milwaukee's Mel Hutchins split the award during the '51–52 season, while Philadelphia's Paul Arizine and Boston's Bob Cousy were co-winners in '50–51. After winning the award, Kidd and Hill hit the road. They appeared on *Good Morning America* and provided studio analysis on TNT during the playoffs. On Memorial Day, Kidd flew to Los Angeles to appear on *The Tonight Show with Jay Leno*. The audience greeted him by wearing Jason Kidd masks.

"He's so down-to-earth and real," Hill said. "We're supposed to be all serious in the days after the award, but we'd wind up giggling at the silliest things all the time. The success definitely hasn't gone to his head."

The award just confirmed what the Mavericks already knew. Jason Kidd was special.

"His statistics are good, but they don't tell half the story," Motta said. "A player like Jason comes along once in a decade.

"Maybe a lifetime."

S EEING STARS

Several Mavericks have taken part in the All-Star Game through the years. Mark Aguirre. Rolando Blackman. James Donaldson.

But Kidd is different. He became the first player in the sixteen-year history of the club to start in the All-Star Game.

The fans had spoken. Kidd received 1,049,946 votes for the 1996 game. Houston's Clyde Drexler was the only guard in the Western Conference with more. Kidd joined Drexler, Houston's Hakeem Olajuwon, Seattle's Shawn Kemp, and Phoenix's Charles Barkley in the West's starting lineup.

This was a big step for Kidd. But it was also a big step for the franchise. Kidd was the first Dallas player to appear in the All-Star Game since

Blackman six years earlier. The team had struggled, winning just eleven and thirteen games in the two seasons before Kidd arrived.

For the first time, the Mavericks had a marquee player. They had hoped that the club was again pointed in the right direction.

"Maybe in four or five years, I'll understand how big it really was," Kidd said. "But right now, this is exciting for me. And my teammates. They're the ones who are responsible for anything I receive."

The Mavericks played the Utah Jazz the night before the All-Star break. Kidd had 20 points and a career-high 25 assists. He led Dallas to a 136–133 double-overtime victory.

The next morning, Kidd flew to San Antonio for the All-Star Game. His flight left Dallas at 10:55 A.M. Kidd arrived at the airport just five minutes before the plane took off.

"I couldn't sleep last night because I was so excited," Kidd said of his first All-Star Game. "By the time I fell asleep, it was time to get up."

Fans swarmed Kidd as he waited for his bags in San Antonio. Fortunately for Jason, a limo provided by the NBA arrived to whisk him away.

Kidd's first stop was a local high school for a rally where some top athletes were invited to talk to students. Kidd was there with Chicago's Scottie Pippen, San Antonio's Sean Elliott, Milwaukee's

Away from the court, Jason loves to relax with a friendly game of golf.

Kidd had 13 triple-doubles entering the 1996-97 season.

Only three active players had more.

Michael Jordan —27
Clyde Drexler —19
Charles Barkley —18
Jason Kidd —13

THREE'S COMPANY

Vin Baker, and track star Michael Johnson. Kidd joked around with Baker before taking the microphone.

"You've got to believe in yourself, and don't let anybody tell you different," Kidd said. "You have to be your own person."

A loud smacking sound echoed in the auditorium. A girl sitting in the first row was blowing kisses at Kidd.

"You're making me blush," Kidd said.

The girl and her friends squealed.

The rest of the afternoon was just as hectic. There was a players' meeting. Kidd and the rest of the All-Stars then met with the media. Seven hours after arriving in San Antonio, Kidd collapsed on his bed in the hotel room. It was his first chance to catch his breath.

It didn't last long. Kidd had to get up and dress for the evening's festivities. He went to dinner with friends. Next was a private party. He returned to his hotel at 1:30 A.M. and asked for a 7 A.M. wake-up call.

Before practice on Saturday, Kidd met actor Will Smith, the group Boyz II Men, and comedian Bill Bellamy. As soon as practice started, Barkley told Kidd that he gets the nameplate over

Jason was on cloud nine *at his first All-Star Game. It surely won't be his last.*

Kidd's locker once the game is finished. It's tradition. Kidd smiled.

"I guess I didn't need to keep that nameplate, after all," he said.

After practice there were more meetings. More autographs to sign. More parties. Kidd was out late again. He was supposed to play golf with Jordan Sunday morning. But both players decided they needed their rest. The match was canceled.

"The weekend probably aged me about two or three years because of the lack of rest, the festivities, and everything going on at night," Kidd said.

Before he knew it, Kidd was sitting in front of his locker at the Alamodome, eating an apple. Barkley's locker was to his left. David Robinson's locker was to his right. The game would start in less than one hour.

If Kidd was tired, it didn't show. His energy and no-look passes in the game's opening moments excited the crowd. He finished the afternoon with seven points and six rebounds in twenty-two minutes. His 10 assists were the game's high total.

The East won the game 129–118. That was the only part of the weekend Kidd would have changed.

"I was on cloud nine," Kidd said. "I'm looking forward to coming back."

Jason bears down on defense against another top, young, NBA point guard — Orlando's magical Anfernee Hardaway.

Jason may be the best rebounding point guard in the NBA.

Asking Kidd to describe what races through his mind as he speeds downcourt is like asking an artist to describe how he paints.

These are qualities that are difficult to articulate. How does someone put their instincts into words? How can someone analyze what their brain processes in a microsecond?

This is Kidd's attempt to depict the string of thoughts on his mind during a fastbreak.

"Once the rebound is determined, I yell for the ball," Kidd said. "My first thought is to turn around and see who's open. That thought goes as fast as anybody can think. The second thought is to push the ball as fast as I can up the court.

"Following that thought is to know who's running with you. Who's on the left wing? Who's behind you? Who's on the right wing? Then, your mind really takes over.

"Who can finish? Who can't? What player will the defense take away from me? Will I have to give it to the trailer?

"All that is probably in a second, a second-and-a-half. Maybe two seconds."

Point guard is more than a position. It's a frame of mind. Sometimes, people wonder how Kidd gets the ball to his teammates. The answer is he doesn't know. Sometimes, in Kidd's own words, "the ball just gets there."

How can anyone pinpoint the qualities that make them special? It's too complex. Or maybe it has to do with being simple.

"I think any player who makes the game simple has a chance to be a great player," Seattle coach George Karl said. "Jason Kidd is a very simple basketball player. He can push the ball. He passes the ball extremely well. He has great defensive hands and he understands defensive concepts.

"He is a great rebounder for a point guard and has some special talents. He makes the game simple for a lot of people."

To Kidd, it's a matter of feel.

"I think it's just a feel for the position you play," Kidd said. "If your mind races that fast, and you're

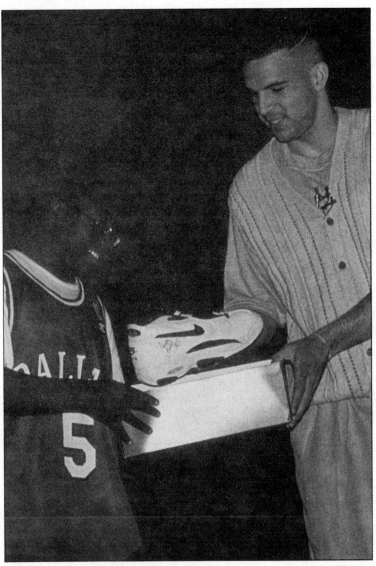

Not all of Jason's assists are restricted to the basketball court. He gives generously to a variety of charities.

able to be successful when you do it, then it's got to be a feeling.

"I guess some people call it an extra sense or extra trait or something. I think it's a combination of God-given talent and just working long hours in the gym. I mean, I don't wake up every day and say, 'I'm glad I can do this or do that.' It takes a lot of hard work."

Even Jason doesn't know how he makes some of his best plays. Sometimes, he says, "the ball just gets there."

Not all of Kidd's assists are restricted to the court. He donated $46,100 to a community church in West Dallas to build a basketball court. He buys a block of thirty tickets to each Mavericks game for underprivileged children. He appears at numerous charity events. He donates $3,500 a year to St. Joseph's in honor of Sal Martinez, a former teammate who was killed in a drive-by shooting. Every Thanksgiving, Kidd and other Bay Area players in the NBA contribute $5,000 to feed the needy in Oakland.

The Future

Kidd has flirted with the idea of playing baseball in the offseason. He stressed this has nothing to do with Michael Jordan's recent attempt to switch sports.

"I would love to try to play in the major leagues," Kidd said. "Not because of Mike. But I think I could be better than Mike. I know I could be better."

Kidd was the center fielder on the St. Joseph team that advanced to the state semifinals his junior and senior years. He hit .333 with 3 home runs and 20 runs batted in his senior year in high school.

When Kidd received a scholarship to the University of California, he was told he could play basketball and baseball if he wanted. He often worked out with Bobby Smith, who is now a shortstop in the Atlanta Braves farm system.

"I would go out and take some batting practice with the fellas to show them I could have played baseball if I wanted, if I put in the time," Kidd said.

He was going to play baseball his sophomore year in college. He decided against it once he declared for the NBA Draft. Kidd was advised not to play to avoid the risk of injury.

The talk of baseball is fun. But Kidd knows his primary sport is basketball. He wants to be at the forefront.

Kidd said he has no problem with Detroit's Grant Hill being the sport's ambassador once Jordan retires. Kidd will be satisfied to be Hill's "vice president or secretary." But above all, he wants to get better.

"Jason is telling everybody that he's still got a long way to go and a lot more to learn," Popeye Jones said. "That's going to be scary five years down the road. It's already phenomenal how well he knows the game and the things he can do on the court."

Jason Kidd loves competition. He hates to lose. Those traits, combined with his exceptional talent, make him one of the game's brightest young stars.

"I know Jason," Payton said. "If he wasn't in the NBA, he'd still play pickup games every day. He loves basketball. It's his first love."

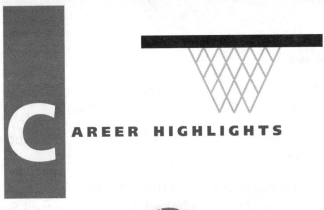

CAREER HIGHLIGHTS

High School

- Led St. Joseph of Notre Dame to consecutive California Division I state titles in 1991 and 1992

- Won the Naismith Award as the nation's top high school player in 1992

- Named the state Player of the Year in 1991 and 1992

- Finished high school career with most assists in California prep history with 1,155

- Played in the McDonald's All-America Game

College

- Only player in University of California history to be named Pac-10 Player of the Year

- Consensus first team All-America his sophomore year

- Led nation in assists (9.1) in 1993–94. That average also established an NCAA record for a sophomore

- All Pac-10 his freshman and sophomore years

- Set Pac-10 season-assist record with 272 in 1993–94

- Led Pac-10 in assists and steals as a freshman and a sophomore

- Set school single-game assist record with 18 against Stanford on Jan. 20, 1994

- Set school career steal record with 204

- Set school single-game three-point record with seven against Washington State on March 12, 1994

- Pac-10 Player of the Week twice in his sophomore year

- Had a Pac-10 record four triple-doubles his sophomore year

Jason hates to lose. Maybe that's what makes him a winner.

- Finalist for the Wooden Award in 1993–94

- Pac-10 Freshman of the Year in 1992–93

- Pac-10 All-Freshman team

- Set Pac-10 single-season steals record with 110. His average of 3.8 steals also set an NCAA freshman record

- Set school single-game steal record with eight against Washington on Jan. 28, 1993

Professional

- NBA Schick co-Rookie of the Year with Detroit's Grant Hill in 1994–95

- Named to the All-Rookie team

- His 13 triple-doubles already ties him for 10th on the all-time list. All of those have come in his last 90 games

- The Mavericks won 23 more games in Kidd's rookie year than the year before. Only three rookies in league history had a bigger impact

- Became the sixth player in NBA history to record at least 700 assists and 500 rebounds in a season. Kidd had 783 assists and 553 rebounds in 1995–96 to join Oscar Robertson, Earvin "Magic" Johnson, Wilt Chamberlain, Norm Van Lier, and Michael Ray Richardson

- First Dallas player to start an All-Star Game, Feb. 11, 1996 in San Antonio

- Averaged a club record 9.7 assists in 1995–96. Utah's John Stockton was the only player in the league to average more

- Topped all guards in rebounding in 1995–96 with a 6.8 average

- Tied for fourth in steals in 1995–96 with an average of 2.16

- Had a club-record and NBA season-high 25 assists against Utah on Feb. 8, 1996

- Named NBA Player of the Week twice in his first two seasons. He joins forward Mark Aguirre as the only two-time winner of the award in club history

- Dallas was 19–9 when Kidd scored 20 or more points in 1995–96

- Named NBA Rookie of the Month for March in 1995

- Led the league in triple-doubles as a rookie with four

- Tied for ninth in the league in assists (7.7) and was seventh in steals (1.91) as a rookie. He was the only rookie to rank in the top 10 in two statistical categories

- Had 10 or more assists in 43 games

- Already ranks among the Mavericks all-time leaders in assists (fifth at 1,390), three-point shots made (sixth at 203) and steals (sixth at 326)

ABOUT THE AUTHOR

David Moore has covered the NBA since the 1983–84 season. He has spent the last seven years as the national NBA writer for *The Dallas Morning News.* Moore's work has been honored by the Pro Basketball Writers Association and the Associated  Press Sports Editors. He has served on the selection committee for the Basketball Hall of Fame and the committee that determines the All-Star ballots. He has served as an analyst on ESPN radio and TV and has written articles for a variety of magazines. This is his first book.

Photo courtesy of David Moore